TOMMY
AND
THE SPIRITS
OF THE AIR

TERRY STEVENS

TOMMY AND THE SPIRITS OF THE AIR

TERRY STEVENS

Lots of Best Wishes
Enjoy the fun

Terry Stevens

ATHENA PRESS
LONDON

ISBN 10-digit: 1 84748 127 2
ISBN 13-digit: 978 1 84748 127 6

First Published 2007 by
ATHENA PRESS
Queen's House, 2 Holly Road
Twickenham TW1 4EG
United Kingdom

Printed for Athena Press

For Kate, Tom and Jessica Berry
With special thanks to Heather and Evelyn

ALSO BY THE AUTHOR

TOMMY, THE WIZARD AND THE MAGIC UMBRELLA

THE BATTLE AT LONGSHORE CAUSEWAY

IN FEAR AND TREMBLING

'No! *Nooo*! I can't go, Mummy!' Little Rebecca Johnson's screams cut through the morning air and resounded around Benshire Close. She was the apple of her mother's eye – a dutiful little eight-year-old who was normally as kind and considerate as she was pretty. She had never been prone to throwing a tantrum or anything else, but now she was growing wild-eyed and desperate as she resisted her mother's pleas to cross the road to Tommy Price's house.

Most Saturday mornings for the past eighteen months, Mr and Mrs Price had looked after Rebecca for the five hours her mother worked, but now her stubborn refusal to move out of her bedroom was causing tempers to rise.

'Why won't you go – what's your reason?' Mrs Johnson's scalp itched as a hot flush burned across her face. Things were getting out of control and she didn't know how to cope. Already she was late and desperate to go, but her wayward daughter was inconsolable and no closer to being brought to heel. Taking a deep breath to ease the pressure of the blood that was throbbing through her dizzy head, she lowered her voice and spoke gently and slowly.

'Darling, please, I love you so much, please tell me why you won't go.'

'Because *he'll* get me, Mummy. He lives there and he *will* get me!'

Jane Johnson sank slowly on to the bed and sat looking into the face of her cowering daughter. The enormity of the words she had just heard buckled her knees and drained the colour from her face. Her whole world had suddenly stopped and her work had lost all importance to her. After a few moments, she rose as if in a trance and walked down the stairs and across the road to the house of Celia Price.

She knocked very quietly, for she was aware that there had been too much noise already in so quiet a street.

Celia opened the door expectantly and showed some surprise at Rebecca's absence. Looking across the Close, she noticed that the door was wide open, but saw no sign of her expected guest.

'Oh dear, is she ill?' asked Celia with concern.

'In a way.'

'What way?'

'She refuses point blank to come.'

'Why?'

'Celia,' Jane lowered her voice to a whisper. 'She says if she comes "he" will get her!'

'Who will?'

'I don't know, I've come to ask you – did someone shout at her? Has she done something to make someone angry at her?'

Celia looked puzzled.

'Not that I know of. She's always so quiet and there's only Tommy and Bill here when she comes. Bill sits doing the cross-word and Tommy's as good as gold with her. They play skipping games and Bill takes them both out with the dog. She came to see the dog yesterday. Jane, she was perfectly happy when she left – she was laughing yesterday. We haven't seen her since. Has she had a nightmare?'

It was a good question and one that had not occurred to the weary mother.

'Hang on,' said Celia, 'I'll just tell Tommy about it – perhaps he knows something.' She ducked inside.

A minute later she reappeared and Tommy was with her.

'Tommy and I will go and talk with her. I'm sure nothing has happened here, Jane. We can't imagine that anyone has upset her. You go to work and we'll go straight across. She will be fine.'

With those words ringing in her ears, Jane set off for the main road and work. Her mind was in turmoil, but she trusted her friend completely and thought she would return home to a more peaceful situation. She was wrong!

In the Dark of the Night

It was in the middle of the afternoon that Jane, exhausted, finally managed to return home. How she had got through the morning she did not know, but her hopes of a happy return evaporated as the grim atmosphere in the house told her all she wanted to know.

Despite all the efforts of Tommy and his mother her little girl was a nervous wreck and remained firmly entrenched in the safety of her bedroom. Celia ushered Jane into the kitchen.

'Jane, I'm going to have to go, but I haven't sorted it out. She's not afraid of Tommy and she's not afraid of Bill, so all that leaves is the dog – and how he's given her the evil eye in the middle of the night the Lord only knows! She's obviously had a terrible night-mare and can't divorce it from reality. Now, I've got her to eat something, but, really, she'll make herself ill, Jane,' Celia said worriedly.

'It's a worry,' agreed Jane, sighing.

Shaking her head, and with Tommy in tow, Celia disappeared back across the road to her poor, neglected husband.

Now, Tommy knew more than almost anything else that Rebecca loved his dog, Patch, with a passion. He returned to Rebecca with his much-loved pooch and found it no surprise that, as he walked his black-and-white companion into her room, her eyes came alive and her arms reached out to the one friend who would never let her down.

As Patch gently licked her face, all the strain and the distress of a long night seemed to melt away. Instead of staring into empty space she was now actually looking into Tommy's eyes and she was seeing him. She was like a little princess who had returned from a nightmare, woken with a kiss from her canine prince.

'Hello, Rebecca.'

'Hello, Tommy.'

Tommy was glad. At that very moment Rebecca was home – his friend had returned to him.

'Did you have a terrible dream?'

'No! I really did see him, Tommy, in the night, when I was watching the moon. It gives off such a beautiful light, so gentle and so warm. It streams in through the darkness and lights up the whole room. Sometimes it is tinged with blue or yellow, but at other times it is pure white; and I see stars hurtling high across the sky, they suddenly shine more brightly than ever and then die in a dazzling burst of light. Then below me, I can see the Close all lit up and sometimes a cat or even a fox will come strolling along. They think there's not a soul awake, but I am, sometimes.'

She looked away and paused, deep in thought.

'I was not asleep,' she said firmly.

'When were you not asleep?'

'Last night. I was not asleep, Tommy, and I saw him.'

She was talking very quietly now. Patch sensed her sadness and rolled over so she could tickle him, but her hands did not move.

'I saw a dark figure, only small, moving quickly across the gardens, keeping close to the shadows so he could not be seen. I was tired and my eyes were closing, but they opened wide as I saw him appear and disappear. He reached your garden. He had his back to me as he opened the front door, but as the light from the hall fell on him, he slowly turned, as if he knew I was watching him and he looked up slowly till our eyes met. The moon was full on my face and he saw me, Tommy. He looked shocked and alarmed and took a step forward to stare hard at me. I dropped the curtains back across the glass and buried myself in the far corner of my room. All night I trembled as I waited for his shadow to fall across my window. He did not come to find me, but he is still there, just across the road, and I dare not walk into his house.'

'Do you mean his house or my house?' asked Tommy, nervously.

Tommy went cold as she gave her reply. 'His house *is* your house!'

FRIEND OR FOE?

Tommy stopped in Rebecca's garden and looked across the road. He had happily believed that some dream-phantom had entered into the little girl's head as she had slumbered in the twilight world between consciousness and deep sleep, but when she screamed, 'The GOBLIN!' in answer to his probing questions, he had been rather taken aback.

The goblin! His mischievous and naughty-looking companion was as lifeless as the wood he had been carved from, and yet...

How many times had he walked into his bedroom to see the goblin slumped against the wall with Patch sat right in front of him, looking into his face, whimpering and wagging his tail, as if longing to continue a quickly cut-off conversation?

Then he recalled wondering what had been missing in the middle of the night when he had got up, all hot and sticky, to get himself a drink. Yes, of course, it had been the goblin. He had been too tired to work out the mystery then, but now he would work it out. He would have no evil spy walking in and out of his house in the dead of the night!

'Uncle Jack?' It was not really a question; Tommy knew who had answered the phone.

'Why, hello, Tommy, how are you diddlin?'

'I'm diddlin just fine, Uncle.' (Tommy's uncle always knew how to talk 'kid's talk' but often he was about five years out of date.)

Tommy cut him well short.

'Uncle, where did you get the goblin?' he asked.

'Oh, isn't that supposed to be my little secret?' said Uncle Jack cheerfully.

'I really need to know, Uncle, please just tell me.'

Taken by surprise, his uncle complied. 'Well, if you must know, I was on the High Street and saw an old toyshop down a narrow alley. I only went to have a nosey, but the shop seemed to draw me in. There was an old lady sat knitting a shawl and the wooden goblin was almost smiling at me. I know you like...'

Tommy didn't hear the rest. He simply put down the phone and walked in a daze up the stairs to stand outside his bedroom door. He opened it slowly to a slight shuffling sound and gazed inside. Nothing moved. The goblin was sitting on the chair.

Tommy knelt before it, face to face, and looked into eyes that refused to move or show any twinkle of life. He drew so close that their faces almost touched and he felt his own breath coming back at him – or was it?

'You have frightened Rebecca half to death. She spent last night and all today hiding in the corner of her room. Is that what you do – put little children in fear of their lives? Are you an evil demon sent to destroy me?' he asked angrily.

The questions continued to come but there was not the slightest response. Tommy lost patience, rose to his feet and threw a blanket over the goblin's head. 'I must be as barmy as Rebecca, talking to a useless lump of wood!' he muttered, and with that he stormed out of the bedroom, slamming the door firmly behind him.

The room shook, and for the next five minutes there was a deathly silence. Then a voice spoke: 'This useless lump of wood needs to breathe!'

With these words, the goblin lifted the blanket off his head and drew in a deep breath. As he looked about the room he quickly drew in another, for there, standing inside the bedroom and looking at him in amazement, was Tommy.

'I thought you had gone,' the goblin said sheepishly.

'Well, I thought you were a harmless toy, so I guess we were both wrong.'

The goblin heard the stern tone in which Tommy addressed him. It was obvious that the boy looked on him with suspicion, perhaps even considered him dangerous. He had not known what to do when Rebecca had seen him, but now he had no choice. He had to try to explain himself and gain the young lad's confidence.

'I am sorry about Rebecca, but really, you don't expect an eight-year-old to be awake at one o'clock in the morning – that is weird! I just didn't know what to do.'

'So you did nothing and left her frightened to death for the whole night!'

The goblin pulled a face.

'So what did you want me to do? Go climbing through her bed-room window and tell her I'm an alien whose been sent from another world and I'm living just over the road? She'd have screamed the house down!'

Tommy could see the sense in the argument. 'So you've been sent from another world – and what world might that be?'

The goblin laughed to himself. 'As if you didn't know!'

Tommy's whole face changed and he stepped much closer. 'Please tell me who sent you.'

The goblin lifted his arms. 'Treen, Queen of the Still High World of Barl.'

Tommy felt a tremendous sense of excitement. 'So you are the companion she promised to send me!'

The goblin looked puzzled. 'She did make a promise to send someone, but it was not as a companion; it was to keep a watch over you. When I spoke to her she decided to send me, but I was not to make contact with you – I was to watch and report... but now you know I am here.'

Tommy was mystified. 'Why do you need to watch and report on me? It's not as if I am going to do anything.'

'Oh, it's not what you are going to do; it's what someone might want to do to you!'

It was Tommy's turn to pull a face; he did not like the sound of that. 'Why would someone want to harm me?' he asked unhappily.

'Because you spoiled his fun. He came to a world that had not fallen, a high world, and spent years getting into the mind of its future queen. He got right into her head and poisoned her thoughts. He made her cold and merciless and then set her upon its throne. The whole world was falling into total chaos, and then...'

'And then what?' Although he had asked the question, Tommy already knew the answer.

'Then you came along, riding like a knight to the rescue on your white horse, and you left his queen, the great Yaar, with all the world of Barl crushed beneath her feet, lying dead under a tree. Then, not content with that, you went and took the shaaf, the great symbol of her power and held it up in your hand! Oh yes, he has really got it in for you and that is why I am here.'

Tommy was in despair. 'I didn't ask to go to your world, and when I got there I didn't really do anything. I just hoped nobody would notice me.'

The goblin looked dumbfounded.

'You hoped nobody would notice you! Are you for real? You came riding in, high up in the sky, the shaaf surrounding you in a circle of brilliant light, and you hoped nobody would notice you? Everybody noticed you!'

'I thought the shaaf was an umbrella! I got it for my birthday, from the toyshop you came from.'

The goblin sat back and raised his eyebrows.

'Well, that just goes to show. There was one extremely bright object up in the sky and one extremely dim one!'

Tommy perceived that the dim one was meant to be him. 'There's no need to be cheeky.' he said. 'Anyway, what does my enemy want to do – kill me?'

'Good heavens, no, he would not be allowed to kill you. His powers are curbed and the Guardians are here to protect you, but they are very busy and Treen is concerned for you – and so am I. So, here I am and I will always protect you.'

Tommy sat down on the bedroom floor and looked with concern at his new-found friend. 'How will I know this enemy and what is his name?' he asked.

'Oh, he comes in many forms, so you may not recognise him, and he has many names, but we know him as the Beast'

Tommy was intrigued and did not understand. 'Surely there was a time when he had one name and he was one person?' he asked.

The goblin looked away as if remembering something long gone. 'Yes, he was Lucifer, one of the greatest and most wonderful of all the angels in heaven, but he got tired of being nice – now, what you see is what you get.'

'So, will I get to see him?' asked Tommy.

The question troubled the goblin. 'I hope not... I really do hope not.' he said, and then quickly changed the subject. 'By the way, you paid three pounds for that umbrella, didn't you?'

'Yes – or should I say my Mother did.'

'Did Treen ever give you the money back?' asked the goblin curiously.

'No.'

'Well isn't that just typical! Still, that's royalty for you!'

THE LIGHT SHOW

Rebecca was eating properly now. Her confidence had returned after Tommy had told her everything about his strange adventure and his even stranger companion, and she had happily believed him. Reassured that the goblin would do her no harm, she had allowed Tommy to carry him over and was now awaiting the show that the little alien had promised to put on for her.

After putting on her favourite music, she settled down to watch as Tommy guarded the door. The goblin stood in the centre of the room and raised both his arms in time to the music. From above her bed Rebecca's favourite toy – a beautiful blue dolphin – rose

gently off the shelf and went swimming around the room, sometimes standing high on its tail in a seeming dance and at other
times diving down towards the floor before quickly rising and
doing double and then treble somersaults.

As he came full circle, a whale joined him and then other fish
who took on vibrant colours as the room glowed in an ocean blue.
Her dolls stood up to watch the whole amazing show as characters
stepped out of her books and danced to the music. Jugglers
juggled, clowns fell about and a whole band marched round,
adding loudly to the music that was already playing.

As the goblin directed his arms towards the window, the curtains
started to glow with a white light, and Rebecca's favourite doll
beckoned for her to go and draw them back. As she did so she was
amazed to see that the early evening moon had drawn close to her
window and his gently smiling face seemed only an arm's reach away.

'You keep smiling and I will keep shining. I am watching over you, my little Rebecca.'

With those words the moon accelerated away till it held its normal position in the sky and its face had faded away. As all went quiet and still behind her, Rebecca excitedly turned to face the room and saw that every toy was back in its normal place with the goblin now lifelessly held in Tommy's arms.

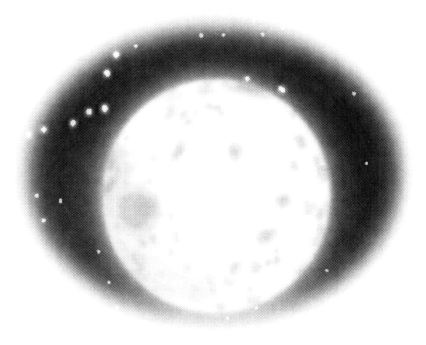

'That music is very loud,' came a voice.

To Rebecca's shock she realised that her mother was standing in the doorway, but it seemed she had seen nothing.

'I had better go now,' said Tommy as he said goodbye and, as she went to follow her mother down the stairs, Rebecca saw the goblin give her a wink and a little wave. When they were back across the road he stood at Tommy's bedroom window and waved goodnight.

Rebecca's neighbour, Mrs Green, who had been clearing away in the garden, walked back into her house and confronted her husband.

'You told me if I stopped drinking I wouldn't see things!' she said angrily.

'Oh Lord, what have you seen now?' he muttered.

'It's that goblin again, only this time he's waving to me from their bedroom window.'

'In that case, you'd better pour me one – and make it a double.' replied her exasperated husband.

Rebecca thought she was far too excited to sleep that coming night, but she actually slept all the way through it.

If only she had stayed awake, she would have seen not one, but two moonlit figures creep silently out of Tommy's house and disappear into the night.

WATCHING THE WATCHERS

Tommy was shocked. Ever since he had returned from the land of Barl he had acted as a magnet for spirits, who flocked to his house to get a glimpse of the little human who had foiled the Beast and set Treen back on Barl's throne. They came disguised in many forms, and it was their comings and goings that had persuaded Mrs Green to come off the drink – and the goblin's comings and goings that had put her back on it!

Now Tommy wanted to see them for himself. The goblin had assured him that they would be in the woods in the dark of the night. He and his little companion had crept into the woods and were now close up by a tree, watching a horde of the little fellows as they milled about and planned their mischief. They were short little creatures with glowing eyes, but their bodies were hard to see in the night.

They were near to a road and suddenly all the spirits held hands in a circular group before lifting slowly into the air. They then started to spin till they hovered high in the sky, taking the form of a flying saucer with its many flashing and coloured lights.

As a car approached, one of the spirits shot down into the engine and, within seconds, the car came spluttering to a jerky halt. Two spirits then started to slowly descend from the ship towards the blacked out car, taking the form of green men with glowing red eyes and horns sticking out of their heads. The driver, trembling, his eyes wild with fear, jumped out of the car and went running down the road back towards the town. The two spirits landed and roared with laughter, dancing a jig.

'Why, the little devils!' said Tommy.

'Yes, well, that's exactly what they are: little devils.' replied the goblin.

As he spoke the whole assembly came back down to earth and collapsed in fits of laughter. It all seemed harmless enough to Tommy, although the poor car driver was now half a mile away and still running like the wind. It wasn't long before the sound of another car could be heard, its engine slowing as it passed the abandoned one that still sat in the road. Two of the spirits immediately got together, one standing on the shoulders of the other, and they walked towards the oncoming car. As it approached they changed into the form of a young girl in a shining white dress and then scattered in two directions as the car went right through them. The driver jumped out of the car and spent a long time desperately looking for the body of the fallen girl in the trees by the side of the road. Eventually two police cars arrived and, as two officers searched, another tried to calm the poor man's wife, who sat crying hysterically in the passenger seat. The officer told her that the road had a reputation of being haunted, which only made matters worse and soon an ambulance had to be called.

The spirits were so convulsed in laughter they failed to notice the goblin and Tommy slip silently away, although one stopped and looked intently at the area where the two had just been.

'The Beast isn't around, so they get up to all sorts of things, but they don't mess about when he's here – he has serious things to do,' the goblin explained.

'So where is he?' asked Tommy.

'Oh, he comes and goes. He's got fingers in all sorts of pies, but he doesn't do the small stuff.'

Tommy was curious.

'What of those little spirits – are they always here?'

'No, they do the planets but the Beast is not allowed to take them past the Edge. Dego is allowed to take him messages in black space, but otherwise, he too is confined. As the corridors to the far worlds start past the Edge, they can't visit them.

Tommy was looking very puzzled.

'Who is Dego and where is the Edge?' he asked.

'Dego is the Beast's commander-in-chief and the Edge starts far past where your sun no longer shines.'

Tommy stopped and knelt down beside the goblin with a mischievous grin spread wide across his face. 'So take me there!' he ordered.

Now the goblin really was alarmed. 'I'm not supposed to interfere. The Wizard interfered and look what happened there!'

'He saved your world,' argued Tommy.

'Yes and then nearly destroyed it by unleashing Yaar on it – non-interference is our absolute rule.'

'Well, it's a bit late for that. I'd say you've interfered already, and so have I. I've been to your world and I've got this Beast thing on my tail. So come on, lighten up. I think it's time you allowed me another trip just to the Edge.'

The goblin was finding it hard to resist the little boy's pleading. After a moment's thought he looked hard at Tommy.

'You are our hero and you are very special, so I will take you to the Edge – but no further, Tommy, not as long as I live will I take you any further.' Tommy smiled for he now knew he could twist the goblin round his little finger! His new adventure was about to really begin.

THE LIGHT BALLS

The goblin had been trying desperately to get out of his promise to Tommy. He knew that once there, Tommy would be able to view deep space and even the slightest glimpse of its wonders might prove too tempting to an Earth boy with his curiosity.

Instead, he had taken him to a place in the dark forest where the light balls came through on an erratic course and at great speed. The small light balls, he told Tommy, enabled him to travel to Barl and back each night. But, in the wood it had proved impossible for them to catch one and the exhausted goblin was now sitting on the ground, puffing and blowing, as Tommy, now weary himself, leaned against a tree; he felt exasperated and suspicious.

'You told me you caught a light ball to get here,' he said, 'so how did you manage it?'

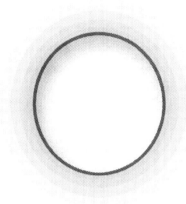

'It's quite simple. Once I step out of the corridor I can see the lights coming toward me. They slow down and turn to head back towards your space on a straight course, so it is quite easy to take one. Then I squeeze it tightly into my hand till it bonds with me.'

To Tommy's amusement the goblin was doing all the actions to accompany his explanation, but his sniggers were ignored.

'Then I open my hand out in front of me and the ball begins its journey back, slowly at first, or so it seems, but soon your sun is shining ever more brightly and a planet of blue with a glowing atmosphere is racing up to meet me. I can turn my hand towards the other planets and view them, but the ball will always return to its earthbound course. Anyway it's best not to hang around when I'm travelling by light ball. Your planet is in the middle of nowhere, way out in the sticks, and it is dangerous, so nobody comes here. When I step out of the corridor I am always on my own; there is nobody to help me. So, be a good boy, play it safe and go back home!'

Tommy was disappointed and started to walk back home. Suddenly, he stopped and turned in his tracks.

'You go back at night, you told me so! You go back to Barl and return before I wake up, so just how do you manage to do that? Answer me, please.'

The goblin couldn't tell a lie.

'I catch them somewhere else,' he said reluctantly, 'where they slow down, just before they lift up into the sky.'

Tommy's eyes opened wide with excitement.

'Where? Where do they slow down?'

The goblin decided to give up his attempt at deceit.

'Where the blue cones fall.'

'The blue cones! I've picked up blue cones… under the conifer, just above the stream.'

Tommy turned and ran. He stumbled and fell in the dark as he tried to find his way to the conifer, but he was soon up as a light ball passed him on its erratic journey.

He tried to chase it but it was soon gone. However, he knew he was going in the right direction. He soon arrived, just as another light ball whistled past, slowed and then shot up high into the night sky.

Tommy could hear the goblin shouting to him from just behind.

'There will only be a few left tonight, most of them have gone. If we miss these we can't go tonight.'

Tommy was determined he would not miss his chance and tensed up as he saw a light zigzagging towards him. Up it went, then down, first to the right and then to the left, till it finally flattened out and slowed to come silently gliding towards him.

Tommy's hand shot out and grasped it, his whole body tingling as its power went into him. Squeezing tightly, he felt the ball sink into his hand and then pull forward, ready to continue its journey.

The goblin easily caught the final ball as it came right up to him, but he looked very sorry for himself as Tommy issued the order to go.

They both opened their hands and felt their feet lift up off the ground as the earth's gravity gave way to a far stronger force. They hurtled up through the Van Allen belts and then past the reflected light of a brilliant moon. Tommy realised the great force that was holding him in full protection was much greater than the light ball he held in his hand.

INTO THE BEYOND

As he looked behind him, Tommy could see that the Earth and the moon were racing away from him, but in front nothing seemed to move. He was looking into a vast black ocean with many distant sparkling and spinning lights, a few of which seemed extremely colourful, but he had no sensation of speed.

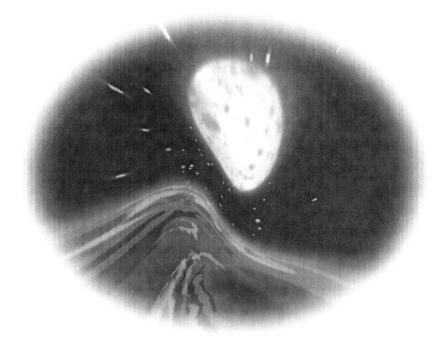

The goblin was close behind him and, as Tommy looked round at him, he realised that the Earth had become a tiny blue speck that would soon be completely gone. The light ball was well set on its course and would have remained so if Tommy hadn't noticed a world far to his left that seemed a dull red but gave flashes of brilliant red as pure, white light illuminated its surface. Long-forgotten words came racing back into his mind… A red-hued paradise, with forests and rivers; it has been turned to dust, its past hidden from human eyes.

Mars! The planet of legend that had fascinated and enthralled the people of Earth for countless generations was now passing him by. This was the planet of 'little green men' who had plotted and planned to make war against Earth from the very beginning of time. How many astronomers had viewed it through their long telescopes and fancied they saw the many canals of a highly advanced civilisation?

Tommy turned his hand and was pulled in a huge arc as the ball obediently turned towards the object of his desire.

Behind him the goggle-eyed goblin, who had been given no time to protest, also turned his hand and went in pursuit of his wayward friend.

It was only after Tommy had arrived at the planet's surface and was racing through the deep, red gorges and along the slopes of its wide-open valleys that the goblin finally caught up with him.

'Tommy, we can't do this.' the goblin shouted. 'We are in normal space time and the night is passing. We must hurry to get to the Edge.'

It was of no use – Tommy was determined to see more, so he raised his hand to lift over a plateau and head out towards an open plain.

Tommy stopped his flight suddenly and gasped. Below him lay a spectacle unseen by human eyes for countless generations.

A FACE FROM THE PAST

Tommy's face turned a ghostly white. Far below, looking silently up at him, was a human face carved into the red rock. It must have stared lifelessly into space through ages now long forgotten, looking hauntingly out towards the Earth and the long-gone civilisation that had left it there. It was of massive proportions, and rose majestically high as if attempting to greet him. It was swathed in the striped headdress of the Egyptian sphinx and Tommy could see carved teeth in the recesses of its mouth.

Could this be the face of an ancient Pharaoh who had ruled the people of a great Martian civilisation?

Tommy looked across the landscape. He saw another object that took his breath away. Far away stood a five-sided pyramid that reached up to the very heavens.

How could an alien world so bleak and so cold have two earth-like structures standing so closely together?

He realised with a start that the goblin was right beside him.

'I never wanted you to see this,' the goblin sighed. 'It was not meant for your eyes – but what could I do? You are so strong-minded, I have been unable to control you.'

Tommy was not interested in the goblin's feeble protests.

'Well I have seen it,' he said shortly, 'so now will you tell me what I am looking at?'

The goblin sighed again. 'You are looking at an area known to your astronomers as Cydonia.' he said. 'Your people have photo-graphed the face – they consider it a natural trick of the light and the shadows. Other structures, such as the pyramid, they consider to have come about naturally, but there are many pyramids. That one over there has four sides and it is massive.'

Tommy followed the goblin's gaze and saw another structure rising high above the plain.

'Was this a Martian civilisation or one alien to the planet?' he asked quietly.

The goblin looked deeply into Tommy's eyes.

'It was an alien civilisation, but it would not have been alien to you, for these are the ruins left by your ancestors. The face and the pyramids and the city were all theirs, this was all part of the empire of the Earth.'

Tommy could only stutter, 'My people were here?'

His shocked expression caused the goblin to continue. 'Yes, your people were here and many people from the far worlds came here to sample the amazing hospitality and kindness of the humans and to stand on this beautiful world. Its rivers ran so deep and so wide and rainbows of glorious colours stretched far across its skies. The trees yielded the most beautiful of any fruits to be found in the galaxies. The fruit of the rose-red patenial plant scented the air for many miles around. A corridor came right up to the face and anyone who stepped out of it would know immediately that they had arrived in the kingdom of the humans. From there they could travel on to the Earth and see the giants that feasted on the leaves of the highest trees and walked in huge herds across its wide-open plains. They could sit high up on the neck of the dinosaur bonehead, or ride between the wings of giant birds. The Great Prince himself loved to walk in the deep lush grass and commune with its people, but the Beast was on the prowl and chose to wage his war upon the earth.

'He brought madness into the minds of those who had walked so peacefully before and turned the place away from the paradise it had previously been.

'So it was that all of humankind returned to the fallen kingdom of the Earth, leaving their travels and their adventures far behind them. The people of the far worlds lost this beautiful Martian sphere. It turned back to the red dust from which it had been formed.

'There is nothing here now, but come with me and I will show you its final wonders.'

As the goblin moved away, Tommy felt a great wave of sadness for all those who had become exiles from this world of dreams.

As they climbed, Tommy saw a huge tear in the landscape, a giant fissure that ran for thousands of miles across the planet's tortured surface. It looked as though the whole planet had been nearly torn apart. Then, the most amazing sight of all came into view.

A giant volcano rose so high that it completely dominated his view, its massive crater looking like a dark abyss that would swallow him into the planet's very soul.

'Your people call it Olympus Mons.' the goblin said. 'It was a great mountain that stood well over twenty miles high, four times higher than the Everest on your Earth. It was the climb of a life-time! People crossed galaxies to stand on its lower slopes and gaze at the vibrant life that filled every corner of the planet. As you climbed, the great firs that rose high above you would soon stand miles beneath you and the dripping plants would give you drinks that tasted of berries and almonds and honey. Now look at it! The madness is complete.

'It was only after everyone had left that the great mountain blew its top, spewing lava and throwing rocks in a most fearsome rage, which pulled Mars apart. As the other mountains joined in unison, so the whole planet turned into an inferno of anger and destruction.

'The Prince himself came to us to give us comfort, but we knew that your world was dangerous now and that our beloved Mars was destroyed. It was home only to dust storms that blew yellow clouds over its devastated surface. There is nothing here now – all that we knew has gone. Now we must also go, but there is great danger on our journey so you must stay with me.'

There was no one to see as two figures streaked high into the sky and headed out to more distant worlds.

THE SILENT KILLERS

As he journeyed forward through space, Tommy was fascinated by a spinning planet, shooting out beautiful colours, which lay some distance off the course he was now being carried. He was so taken by this distant object that he noticed nothing else.

Suddenly his arm was almost pulled out of its socket as the light ball in his hand violently veered off its course and hauled him upwards and to his right, zigzagging and turning sharply left as two huge rocks zoomed within metres of his terrified face. From nowhere and within moments his adventures had turned into the stuff of nightmares!

Only seconds after completely obscuring his view, the rocks moved away, like two silent assassins, doing cartwheels as they travelled on at tremendous speed to continue their never-ending journey around the sun.

'We're in the asteroid belt,' shouted the goblin, 'so say your prayers.'

The words were of little comfort to Tommy. He had not had time to say anything as the rocks had nearly taken his head off!

After that the light balls seemed to take evasive action much sooner, pulling them both on to different courses whenever a dark object appeared in their view.

Soon the goblin became more relaxed and shouted across to Tommy. 'The belt's behind us now. That's Jupiter ahead – one of the two gas giants of your solar system, but we can't go near it; it's lethal.'

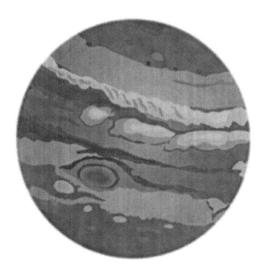

Tommy could see the planet more clearly now. It had bands of yellow and gold with white clouds shooting across the surface and a huge red spot that seemed to swallow the clouds up and then throw them back out again.

He could see dark spots travelling across the surface of the

planet – they must be moons – and hear crackling like a radio that was not tuned to any particular band.

'The light balls will take us past at a safe distance.' explained the goblin. 'That great red spot is three times the size of your Earth and is a storm that has raged for centuries. It is the greatest storm in the universe.'

'You've seen the whole universe?' Tommy asked hopefully.

The question agitated the goblin.

'No, I haven't seen the whole universe – but who has?' he said sulkily. 'It is expanding all the time so you can never get to the end of it.'

'What is it expanding into?'

The goblin looked puzzled so Tommy explained further.

'If the universe is expanding, it must be expanding into something.'

Now the goblin really was agitated.

'Oh, I don't know. I've never thought about that.'

'Oh, so you're not as clever as you think, or I'm not as stupid,' said Tommy smugly.

The conversation was beginning to alarm the goblin and he tried to reassert control.

'Look, we can't go any closer. Jupiter's radiation belts are 10,000 times more intense than those that surround Earth and we could not survive them. The power needed to protect us would itself tear us apart. We are only flesh and blood.'

'Well, I am, but you're not – you're just a lump of wood!'

The goblin exploded.

'Oh, Tommy, you've got to be joking. You can't be that thick! You think I'm made out of wood?'

'Well you look like it to me.'

The goblin shook his head.

'You're either taking the Mickey or you've learned nothing – you must be taking the Mickey!

Tommy hadn't been, but he just smiled and said nothing.

The goblin looked at him in a strange way, as if his feelings had been hurt.

They were no longer like two friends who were totally at ease with each other; there was an awkwardness between them.

Tommy wondered if there was more to this friendship than met the eye. Would he ever really know if he could trust this unknown friend with his life – and what if he couldn't? He suddenly felt very alone.

'Jupiter is your sentinel,' the goblin said kindly, 'your planet's guardian. Its mass and gravity draw in rocks that would otherwise eventually crash into the Earth. It is your friend – as I am!'

The goblin was speaking kind words designed to recreate trust, but Tommy's thoughts were darker than before. He had deliberately tested the goblin's patience and found it to be wanting. The light balls powered up and they were quickly pulled away to leave the giant of the solar system far behind them.

A WONDER IN THE DARKNESS

There would never be another moment in Tommy's life that would affect him like this one. Almost 1 billion miles into space and with Jupiter far behind him, he came to the second giant, a planet so magnificent that for a moment he was unable to speak. He drew his hand into his chest and hovered in the ever-increasing cold and darkness to look upon a wonder he would never have imagined to be there.

Saturn! Filling all of space before him – a yellow ball of gas that was surrounded by layers of rings so perfectly knitted together that they encircled the planet as one. What mighty creator had fashioned such a majestic monument to both his power and the genius of his mind?

Tommy spoke aloud. 'Did a great spiritual being form this in an age long gone from us now, so that he would never be forgotten after he had faded and died?'

'Well, you're half right, but the "faded and died" part is a bit dramatic,' answered the goblin. 'The power that created this is the same power that has brought you here and he is holding you in his hand!'

This was just too much, far too fantastic for Tommy to believe. Why would someone with so much power be using it on him?

The goblin could see his bewilderment.

'Tommy, if it were not for him your feet would never have left the ground, you would still be walking in the woods. It is not just little spirits that are interested in you.'

As Tommy listened he felt drawn to go closer to this beautiful sphere, so put out his hand and felt a tug as he was pulled nearer still.

'Can I stand on its surface?'

The goblin smiled. 'It has no solid surface, and the winds howl at thousands of kilometres an hour, so you would be blown clean back to the Earth. Mind you, that might not be a bad idea.'

But Tommy had stopped listening. His attention had been drawn to something very strange. Little black spots were shooting off the rings and out into space before stopping and quickly heading back. Then they clambered back on to the tumbling rocks before a collision would throw them off again. It was like a fairground carousel in which the rocks were the horses. Riding them were the same spirits he had seen in the woods and their forms were becoming very clear to him now. As he surveyed the scene he was totally unaware that one figure had been thrown into a dark space not far from him, but instead of turning to go back, it was floating with its mouth wide open and its red eyes glowing like embers in a fire. Then it lifted its head and a terrible wail, a cry that chilled Tommy to his bones, filled the whole of space.

At this chilling sound, hundreds of creatures came like bullets to fill the space around Tommy and the scorn and the smirks that came on their faces told him all he needed to know.

'When I give you the shout, open your hand out completely in front of you and bury your head in your chest,' the goblin whispered frantically, his face turned so the spirits could not see his lips move.

'Run, run to the far reaches. *Now*!'

With the light balls at full power, both Tommy and his protector passed the spirits in such a blur of speed that not one of them had time to move, they simply turned their heads after the event and watched the light trails as they powered away towards the Edge – but they had all recognised Tommy, although his strange companion was completely unknown to them. Now they were asking themselves one question: where to lay the trap? They knew that Tommy, at least, would have to come back their way again if he ever wanted to get home.

Now far away, the distraught goblin and a bemused Tommy were hanging on for dear life as their incredible speed left the silent worlds of Uranus and then Neptune deep in their wake.

Tommy had tried to sneak a look at the deep, blue grandeur of the swirling water world of Neptune and its white frozen moon, but it was gone in a blink. They only slowed when the sun had become little more than the distant flame of a candle and the tiny ice world of Pluto, with its circling moon, had come quickly upon them.

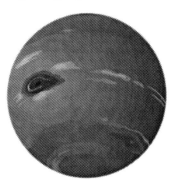

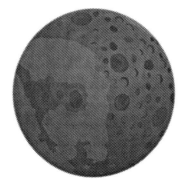

STRANDED

Tommy could see that the goblin was more frightened and worried than ever and this was making him feel uneasy. Hovering in a cold and dark outpost of space with only a tiny ice world and its moon for company, they could both see that the sun, although still bright, was a tiny speck billions of miles in the far distance.

The goblin's argument was that it was all taking too long and the distance still to travel to reach the Edge was daunting. With a small army standing between them and the Earth, and the night passing quickly away, surely it was time to turn back.

'The dark side of the Earth will soon be turning back into the sun and it will be seen that you are not in your bed, Tommy.' said the goblin. 'Help me plan how to get back safely and I will take you on other adventures – although they will take place much closer to your home!'

The begging tone of the goblin's pleas made Tommy's heart sink. He still longed to journey on, but if he did, would his anxious companion be sure to follow and what further dangers could be hiding in the darkness of space? If he travelled on alone would he recognise the Edge when he reached it, or the corridor, which the goblin had been so reluctant to describe? He had been told how to open his hand to let the light ball go but that was only meant to happen on his return to Earth. What if he opened it when he thought he had reached the corridor? He would either be pulled in to be transported to new worlds or left stranded to drift helplessly and lost for the whole of eternity. The risk was too great.

Once Tommy had agreed to go back, the goblin was all smiles as he thought out their situation and tried to plan their safe return.

'Tommy, the spirits are at Saturn, so if we open our hands we will be past them before the light balls start to slow down. If we then hide in the woods and detour away from the road, we can get you back home.'

Tommy had a better idea.

'Why not stay at full speed all the way? Then they would never catch us.'

Tommy's enthusiasm made the goblin smile.

'Well, they would certainly never catch us, but I would like to keep my teeth in and hitting the earth at 1 million miles a second would not be helpful! Anyway, the light balls always slow down on the final approach; you can only control them on the journey.'

Their course of action now decided, the two tiny figures put their heads in their chests, opened their hands to the distant sun – and did not move an inch!

Tommy looked around and then tried again, but the goblin looked dismayed and put his hand to his side. 'I forgot!' he said in despair. 'The light balls are on a circuit. They will not turn back till they have reached the corridor that lies past the Kuiper belt and far outside the solar system.'

'Well that's fine,' said Tommy. 'We'll just keep going. Once they've completed their circuit the light balls can take us back to earth.'

The goblin shook his head. 'You don't understand. The Kuiper belt is the hardest journey of all. To endure it twice, just to end up back where we are now, would be extremely foolish… though it appears we have no choice!'

'What is the Kuiper belt?' Tommy was curious.

'It is an area full of moving objects. Some are dwarf planets and others are more like icebergs, but they are dangerous and as it is so dark and dim many of them come on you unseen. However, we won't be doing the steering, so it's a case, really, of hanging on for our lives! Once we are through, the light balls go at tremendous speed to the corridor and then turn round and come back. So, if you're ready, let's go.'

Tommy liked the idea of getting to the corridor, but he was not so keen on the idea of coming back. And as he started to glimpse the wonders of deep space, he decided *his* light ball would be coming back on its own!

NOW IT BEGINS

Ahead of them both, Tommy had seen a single light ball travelling steadily into the centre of what appeared to be a ring of red-and-yellow gas that gave entrance to a lighter and bluer space than they had seen before.

He could hear the goblin shouting to him, 'That's the Helix Nebula. Once through the centre, the corridor is on the other side. Stay as you are and the ball will turn back through the ring and head towards your sun. We go back non-stop, so remember to let the light ball go when it slows in the woods and then hide in the trees. I'll see you there.'

Tommy was hardly listening. He was now gliding right through the centre of the massive circle and could see the solitary light ball in front turn and head towards a dark circular tunnel which it passed very slowly before speeding up and racing back through the ring.

His light ball was now on its approach and had slowed down to a crawl.

Tommy quickly took his chance, opening his hand and blowing on the ball till it parted from him and then continued on its way. He was then gently drawn into the corridor's entrance and was just being pulled more quickly when he noticed that the goblin had come up beside him.

The little man of wood was protesting furiously, but his movement seemed distorted and slow and his speech was slurred so that Tommy could not understand him.

As they moved at blurring speed, Tommy noticed they were passing other corridors of various colours that were linked to the main corridor, but ran off in different directions. Sometimes they

slowed down dramatically as they passed them, allowing Tommy a tantalising glimpse of other worlds at their far end.

Suddenly he and the goblin shot off down a yellow corridor and in moments found themselves standing on a new world. As they steadied themselves, Tommy looked hard at the goblin preparing to defend his action fiercely, but his heart sank as he realised that the little fellow was sobbing. The goblin was inconsolable. Tommy had got what he wanted, but he realised that by so doing he had hardened himself and become cruel and thoughtless. He put his arms around the goblin and embraced him warmly to try to stop the crying. This stopped the tears. 'I am sorry!' he exclaimed. 'I hate to see anyone cry.'

'But you don't even trust me, Tommy,' the goblin protested, 'so I don't know what to do. You want to prove yourself stronger than me, and you are! I didn't come to watch over you because I'm braver or stronger, but because I care.'

The words so touched him that Tommy decided to show more friendship and a little more trust. So, hand in hand, they walked down the path on the world of Sestar to see the funniest alien Tommy was ever likely to meet.

MEETING BANAL BNAN

'You must meet Banal Bnan – he beats his mother.'

'He beats his mother!' Tommy was seething.

'Yes, he beats her at every game they play. He just can't stand to lose. If he *does* he tries to smile, but his lips are tight and you can hear his teeth grinding! He played his mother best out of three, but when she won two he changed it to the best out of five. By midnight he had made it the best out of thirty-seven and his mother was so tired she was in tears, so they called it a draw! He knew he had lost really and spent the night unable to sleep. The next morning he couldn't eat his breakfast and sulked all day. His mother never dared to beat him again; she was afraid he'd starve to death.' The goblin was in fits of laughter, but Tommy was very angry.

'I think Banal Bnan needs to be taught a lesson,' he declared.

'Do you? Oh well, if you can teach Banal Bnan a lesson, you're a better man than me. Mind you, you are a better man than me, of that there can be no doubt.'

As they talked, they sauntered through a beautiful world with a bright yellow sky and waterfalls cascading down thousands of metres into rivers that flowed to a crystal-clear lake. The air was so crisp and fresh that it tingled in Tommy's lungs and made his whole body feel more vibrant and alive.

As he was taking in both the air and the beauty, he noticed two figures coming down the road to meet them. One was tall and beaming with a silly grin and was waving his arms, while the other was much shorter and looked rather serious.

'The tall one is Banal Bnan and the other one is his friend, Kpump,' the goblin told Tommy, whispering, as if passing on a great secret.

Kpump came right up to Tommy. '*Hallo! Guten tag! Wie geht es ihnen?*' Kpump looked at Tommy expectantly, but Tommy simply looked straight back at him.

After a moment, Kpump tried again. '*Klasse! Auch gut. Das ist mein freund, Bnan.*'

Still no reply from Tommy, not a sausage. The guy was getting agitated.

'*Mein name ist Kpump.*'

By this time Bnan was on the floor in stitches and it was obvious Kpump was getting very annoyed. He shouted in exasperation as he tried to make himself understood.

'*Ich spreche Deutsch. Wir wollen eine party feiern. Hast du lust zu kommen?*'

Again the question was met with total silence.

'*Das darf doch wohl nicht wahr sein!*' and with that final sentence, Kpump shrugged his shoulders, turned around and walked off.

Bnan was laughing so much he was in pain. 'He just said "unbelievable" but I told him to learn English. You'll never get a German out here, only a mad dog or an Englishman! So, how are you, Shekencha? Lovely to see you again, darlin'.'

Tommy's mind was whirling – Shekencha, so that's the goblin's name, but I hope Bnan doesn't call me darlin', the big Jessie!

As he thought it he noticed Bnan shot him a glance. Oh no, I hope he can't read my mind!

'Oh, don't worry, I can't read your mind,' Bnan said almost instantly.

'Thank goodness for that,' Tommy replied, but then stood there looking extremely puzzled.

'Don't call me Shekencha, just call me Goblin!'

Bnan smiled, 'Oh, all right Gobbo, but you'd better introduce me to your friend. He is an Earthman, isn't he?'

Tommy introduced himself. 'My name is Tommy and, yes, I am from Earth. It is very nice to meet you, Banal.'

At the name, Bnan's eyebrows went up and down like pistons and Tommy could hear his teeth grinding.

'Banal, eh? So who told you my name was Banal?'

He was shooting glances at the goblin, but the little guy was so mortified he looked away.

Bnan spoke slowly, 'Do you know that Banal means the pits, a low life, somebody you'd find in the gutter!'

'Oh no, I didn't,' replied Tommy coldly, 'I thought it meant a bad loser or somebody who can't stand to be beaten by his own mother!'

The goblin was nearly choking and the smile had been wiped off Bnan's face.

'Oh, so you've been told that I'm a bad loser, have you? And you know about my mother, do you? So it's like that is it?' he shouted.

The goblin was pulling such excruciating faces that Tommy wondered if he was in pain.

'The gardens are looking lovely at this time of the year,' the goblin said suddenly, 'and your garden is beautiful. What a lovely garden you keep, Bnan, so full of stunning colours.'

Bnan was distracted. 'Well thank you, Gobbo. I do my best, and it is the competition next week so I've been really busy.'

'Yes, well I think you will win it again, Bnan, you'll be very hard to beat.' Bnan was still looking menacingly at Tommy, but his garden was his pride and joy and such praise meant he was prepared to forgive, although to forget would be quite a different matter!

Tommy's Great Challenge

On the walk to Bnan's house, Tommy noticed people and animals in a lush green area with a brown track running around it that probably covered about two miles. Four hundred metres from a starting point was a yellow area with a blue pole, but the track continued past this to run in a huge sweep to the left till it finally returned to the start. The track rose and fell in several places and looked very hard work for any animal given the task of racing round it.

Bnan noticed Tommy looking.

'That's the Place of Challenge, but there's very little point as the champion is so good he never gets beaten.'

'Yes, he's amazing' interrupted the goblin. 'He's so good he's had a mirror put on one of the bends so he can see himself as he runs past.'

'Yes, well, I do look rather grand,' smiled Bnan.

'So you're the champion!' spluttered Tommy.

'Yes, of course, who did you think? And, I never back down from a challenge.'

'Never back down from a challenge – then that's what you've got! I challenge you.'

Bnan was shocked. 'You're having a laugh!'

'We'll see whose having a laugh!' Tommy was determined to teach this bad loser a lesson.

The goblin was frantically shaking his head but Tommy took no notice. So down they went to the Place of Challenge. A crowd quickly gathered at the sight of Bnan, the great champion.

'The winner is the first to touch the pole, but I can't win unless I overtake you in the yellow area, so you must remember that – and don't forget: he who hesitates has lost!'

'Does that mean you are going to give me a lead?' Tommy asked.

'Yes, I'll give you more of a lead than you could ever dream, but I'll still catch you,' Bnan said mockingly.

Tommy was determined that he would not!

They lined up and waited for the start as a huge crowd chatted excitedly.

'Ready, steady, go!' The starter's flag fell, but Tommy hesitated as Bnan raced off at a frantic speed. The champion was soon in a huge lead.

Much to Tommy's surprise, Bnan did not stop before he reached the yellow area but continued on past it without touching the pole and then swerved to the left, only slowing to look at himself in the mirror as he went past. He then raced on round the huge track, speeding up as he ran ever faster, till a cloud of dust was being thrown up from his feet.

Tommy realised that Bnan was not so much ahead of him now as behind him. In fact, he was fast finishing the whole two mile circuit and would soon be back past the start and racing to beat Tommy to the pole.

By now panicking to cover the last 100 metres and reach the pole first, Tommy entered the yellow area desperately reaching out his hand as a now slowing Bnan came thundering past to touch it first.

It was some time before the overheated little boy could even speak.

'I don't think that was fair. Your legs are much longer than mine,' complained Tommy.

The fact that Bnan had run two miles more was never mentioned.

'Well, if you are worried about long legs you can race Linny on the sluppery; he's only got little legs.'

That sounded a much better idea, so Tommy was led to a small gooey hill surrounded by a gooey lake. Competing against him was a little fellow that looked like a duck. Although the creature only had short legs, Tommy noticed that its feet were webbed and wondered if that would give it an advantage.

As the crowd gathered round, Bnan gave Tommy his instructions.

'The sluppery is very thick so you won't sink: just race on it round the island and get back here as quickly as you can. Do not go on to the island and keep your mouth shut.'

'Keep my mouth shut indeed! I think you've got a cheek!'

Bnan looked shocked but repeated himself loudly, 'Just keep your mouth shut.'

As the flag fell a deeply insulted Tommy raced onto the sluppery, but as he tried to turn left his feet went from under him and he ended up sliding flat on his face on to the island and halfway up the gooey hill. As he tried to stand up, he fell again and went sliding back down the hill, face-first in the sluppery. He arrived at Bnan's feet choking, with his mouth full of the gooey stuff.

Bnan tried to help by slapping Tommy on his back so he could breathe again.

'I told you to keep your mouth shut!' he scolded him.

After Tommy had recovered, he was given the bad news.

'You did arrive back first, so well done on that, but as it was on your face and you did not go round the island, you lost – so it seems I win again!'

'Oh no you don't!' Tommy wasn't having *that*. 'I didn't race you; I raced Linny, so Linny won.'

'Well, yes, in a way, but Linny is my champion and was racing for me, so, under the rules, I win. Now that makes two, so all that leaves is the challenge of the birds.'

'Lead me to 'em!' roared Tommy defiantly.

THE TWO OSTRICHES

Without a doubt the little lad's determination had won admiring glances from the crowd. Bnan was concerned that the Earth boy was completely covered in sluppery and suggested he cleaned himself first. So as Bnan washed all Tommy's clothes in the river and squeezed them to quickly dry in the warming sun, Tommy showered himself on the edge of one of the huge waterfalls not far from the track.

Everyone in the crowd had moved away to afford him his privacy, but the goblin was nearby and blushed as he quickly looked away. No one noticed, other than Bnan.

Once Tommy was dry and had put on his slightly damp clothes, he walked with Bnan towards the crowd and two birds that were nestled side by side at the track.

Tommy instantly recognised them as ostriches from his native Earth, but Bnan was at pains to point out that they were not.

'They are similar to your ostriches and they, too, can run very fast – faster than your horses.'

'Is that a fact?' countered Tommy. 'Then I shall look forward very much to seeing an ostrich win the Grand National!'

A huge grin spread across Bnan's face and he roared with laughter. He laughed so much that tears were rolling down his face and Tommy could not help but smile.

'An ostrich winning the Grand National!' Bnan was on his knees. 'You Earthmen! So that's your sense of humour, very dry. My word, meeting you is turning into quite an experience!'

Still grinning, Bnan explained the rules of the final race to his brave opponent.

'To make you feel at home we will call these birds ostriches. As challenger, you choose your ostrich, and then sit on its back. You have the advantage as you are much lighter than I am, so your ostrich should win. To get them to rise up, you rub them under the chin and to get them to run faster, you rub them on the neck. Got that? Up – chin, faster – neck. Once round the track and back to here and the crowd's decision is final. May the best ostrich win!'

To Tommy's surprise, his ostrich rose up the moment he had got on its back and before he could rub it under the chin. Bnan's did the same. The ostriches then trotted up to the line and all went quiet.

'Ready… hold them birds steady… Go!'

Bnan's ostrich set off like greased lightning and was halfway to the pole before Tommy's had even started. In desperation he started to rub the bird's neck frantically and it soon responded with a fierce gallop. Unfortunately for Bnan he slowed his bird down at the mirror so he could have a look at himself and this

helped Tommy to catch up. By the time they reached the hilly parts of the track, Bnan's weight was starting to tell and Tommy's bird surged past him.

One in the eye for Bnan, thought the excited little boy.

Up at the finish, the goblin was jumping up and down and the whole crowd were roaring their approval – this would be Tommy's finest hour! But it was not to be. Just as the finish was within his grasp he saw the whole crowd look up to the sky and let out a huge roar. Over his head, its wings flapping furiously, and with Bnan rubbing fiercely under its chin, flew the other ostrich, only to come down quickly and land with its legs a blur as it crossed the finishing line in front of him.

The crowd raced to Bnan and hoisted him high on to their shoulders to carry him in a triumphal procession back towards his house.

'But ostriches can't fly,' screamed Tommy.

'I told you they are not ostriches,' shouted Bnan. 'If you'd rubbed it under the chin to go up, you'd have beaten me. Now, everyone, back to my house for tea!'

Tommy clambered off his ostrich sadly as the goblin danced past.

'Come on, Tommy, it's party time!' But a party was the last thing that Tommy wanted!

The Final Goodbye

Everybody went up the hill to Bnan's house. Once there, many of them sat down in his beautiful gardens while others went into the house to greet his mother and his sister.

Tommy was welcomed warmly by his host and put in a seat of honour next to the goblin where he could be seen by many of the guests. Bnan and his sister were busy for hours, bringing out all kinds of bread and cheeses with beautiful fruits and creamy-layered cakes. Some of the guests helped in bringing out jugs full of different coloured juices and some carried jugs full of hot, sweet tea.

Tommy became very annoyed when he noticed that Linny was waddling around behind Bnan as if he was his pet. 'So the two of them are in league with each other; I should have guessed,' he muttered to himself.

The goblin had noticed Tommy's frowns and leaned over. 'You don't get it do you?' he asked.

'I don't get what?' growled Tommy.

'Bnan was told you were coming, so he prepared this whole party just for you and has made you his guest of honour. He has spent two days inviting everyone to his house and working hard gathering and crushing many fruits for their juice, while his mother and sister made the cakes and went to exchange baked goods for cheese. The smell that fills the whole house is from the last of the bread which they have just lifted from the ovens. Now, Bnan is doing all he can to get his mother to rest, fluffing up her cushions and pouring her out the nectar of the strawbear tree.'

'But he is such a bad loser,' moaned Tommy.

'A bit like you, do you mean?'

The goblin's argument made Tommy give a huge sigh as he realised it was true. He *was* a bad loser!

'Look,' the goblin continued, 'everybody knows Bnan does not like to lose and will do everything he can to beat them, but they don't mind. He is so good and so kind to everyone that he meets and he would never deliberately hurt anyone. He is one of the nicest people you will ever meet and they regard it as an honour when he beats them. Is that too much to ask?'

At that very moment, Bnan raised a glass to his special guest and everyone, inside and out, stood up to toast their first ever Earthian guest.

'Who told Bnan that I was coming?' asked Tommy, once all the cheering was over.

'The one who brought you,' said the goblin. 'Your visit is the first step towards reunification, the first move towards the Earth and all the worlds once again becoming one.'

Much later, after all the music and the singing and dancing had ceased, it was time for Tommy and the goblin to resume their journey. As he said goodbye to Bnan, Tommy felt very sad and very down. Still, if he was to be instrumental in bringing the Earth back into unity with this other world, then perhaps he would see Bnan again soon.

'Alas,' said Bnan, 'we will not meet again soon. It will be a long road and far into the future before we do, but fate decrees that we will stand together as brothers on new worlds. Till then, may the Mighty One and the Great Prince protect you on all your journeys. Goodbye my new-found friend and my brother.'

As he re-entered the corridor, Tommy had Bnan's whispered words to the goblin ringing in his ears.

'Follow your dream, Shekencha, follow your dream.'

The goblin had half-smiled on hearing those words but had also looked awkward and embarrassed. Tommy wondered what the goblin's dream was.

THE ISLAND AT THE CENTRE OF THE UNIVERSE

Tommy noticed that the goblin seemed more relaxed now. The fact that Bnan had been expecting them had taken away his anxiety and he seemed content to be taken wherever the path would lead. But stroking Linny had reminded him of his dog, Patch, and he was picturing him now, standing at the top of the stairs with his head cocked to one side in puzzlement as he watched both of his friends walk out of the front door and one probably out of his life for ever.

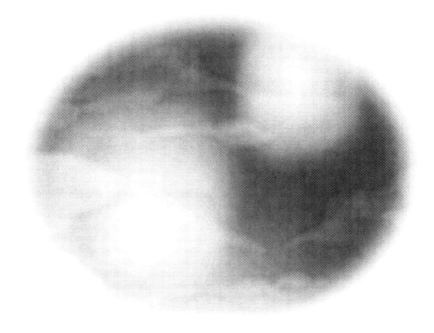

Tommy knew that the end of this adventure might also be the end of the goblin's watch over him. As neither he nor the goblin could talk to each other during the journey, he contented himself with his thoughts as they rejoined the main corridor and hurtled past junctions and intersections till they were finally pulled into a deep blue corridor that seemed to turn them on their heads, till they finally stepped out on to an amazing new world.

Both of them stood transfixed at the sight of two distant suns occupying one planet's sky. Neither of the suns seemed to give out a particularly strong light or heat, but between them they coped admirably. Before them stretched flat meadowland covered in flowers, but there were no signs of animals or any alien life forms.

Tommy turned to follow blue beams of strong light that seemed to come from neither sun, when he saw a huge circular floating island that hovered miles over his head. The light came from every direction and seemed to be focused right on the island.

When the goblin looked up he was beside himself with excitement and became so animated he almost broke into a dance.

'Tommy, I can't believe it, this is the Planet of All Knowledge and that is the mystical Isle of Pacha. Once you ascend its heights you don't need to visit the universe, the universe visits you! Images of planets and people are beamed into your mind. You can visit the greatest wonders of interstellar space without ever leaving here. To come and visit is by invitation only and many wait a lifetime but are never given the call. We are so deeply honoured, it is beyond belief!'

As he was speaking, two radiant aliens stepped out of the corridor and walked towards the isle. As they did so they were lifted up and floated in rapture till they were placed on its gentle grass.

Tommy and the goblin quickly followed. They felt a gentle hand lift their bodies high up into the sky and as they landed they saw the two aliens already in a trance and floating in the clear blue light.

As they, too, were lifted into the light they felt a mighty spirit's peace and love fill their minds and then they started to see some of the stunning worlds that he had created. It was in these moments that they found the perfect beauty and perfect goodness of an eternal creator. In all his works he had sought only to create visions of wonder that would bring rapture to the hearts of all who saw them.

Tommy's eyes had never seen and he had never imagined the things he was seeing now. Yet, strangely, as he came to the end of his visions, the one planet he chose to visit was one that he felt was tinged with overwhelming sadness and terrible despair. How he would be taken there he did not know, but the promise had been made to him while in his trance and he knew it would be kept. The goblin had also been made a promise… to visit the most beautiful world in the universe.

Then they both noticed a huge shape come slowly circling in from high in the sky. It glided on huge, outstretched wings to land far down on the plain.

'That's our ride, Tommy; it's an inter-galactic bird that has been sent for us. This is the adventure of a lifetime!'

With that, the goblin stepped off the isle and floated down toward the bird. Tommy stepped off after him with great trepidation.

If this was a dream, Tommy hoped he would never wake up.

THE BACK OF BEYOND

In a galaxy seventy-six light years from our own, a glorious star had started to burn too brightly. On its final day, looking at its most majestic, and taking several nearby worlds to their grave with it, it suddenly exploded, a supernova that would light up the skies of distant inhabited planets for many years to come.

After it had cooled, the star was no longer bright or burning. It became a small, spinning ball of black matter, unseen in the darkness of space. On a nearby charcoal world only just spared total destruction, a dark figure sat in total isolation. This was his kingdom, a place of gloom and few shadows, the only light glimmering palely, coming from a far-distant star. This cold, dark place was his chosen abode; although legend has it that he was imprisoned in a land of fire and brimstone.

He had once been told that fire would be the cause of his demise, so he tried not to let the light of it sparkle too often in his red-hued eyes. A tiny figure came rushing into his domain, only slowing to bow and grovel before him as its eyes became accustomed to the gloom.

'My Lord, we have seen the Earth boy, Tommy,' squeaked the demon.

The look he received on giving the news made him tremble in fear.

'So! You've seen Tommy, how amazing! I haven't seen him myself since yesterday,' growled its master.

'But we have seen him in the solar system, sire.'

The creature leaned forward in total disbelief. 'You've seen him in the solar system – Earth is in the solar system, so what's new?'

'What is new is that we were at Saturn at the time, my Lord.'

'So your eyesight's improved!'

'It didn't need to, sire, he was at Saturn too.'

Glowing eyes fixed themselves harshly on the unwelcome intruder.

'Were you riding the rings?'

'Yes, sire.'

'I see, and one of the rocks went and hit you on your head?'

'No, sire, we all saw him… and a wooden goblin.'

The frightened little demon was beginning to realise how ridiculous his story sounded and the fearsome sight of his furious master rising up before him was getting too much to bear.

'Dego, have you left the whole legion with no commander to come and tell me *this*?' roared his master.

'They are at Mars, sire, waiting for the boy's return.'

The roar that followed shook his whole body. He turned to escape the destruction that was about to come upon him.

Far behind Dego, the Beast sat back down on his throne to think about the situation.

Tommy was earthbound – but hadn't he also been earthbound before he was transported to Barl? And a goblin… what utter nonsense! Still, he had better go and ask some questions, for if Dego had indeed gone mad, then he must be relieved of command. The creature left his domain and headed for white space.

ON A WING AND A PRAYER

As Tommy approached the magnificent bird it lifted its head and let out a most terrifying cry. Startled, he quickly stepped back and nearly fell over the goblin, who was now walking behind him. Looking up, he saw that the bird's call had been to another of its kind, which had just entered the skies and was circling in to pick up the two smiling aliens, who were not far behind.

The bird put its wing flat to the ground so that Tommy could climb aboard and he was soon seated on its neck with the goblin holding on tightly to his waist. The bird raised itself up and started to run, beating its wings slowly; soon it lifted its feet and rose gently into the sky. As they circled the Isle of Pacha and viewed the planet's distant horizons, the bird made powerful downward thrusts on its wings that lifted it quickly and at much greater speed till it burst out of the planet's lower atmosphere and up to the very edge of space.

As Tommy and the goblin sat glued to the gigantic creature, it skimmed the little air that was left, took a last gigantic intake of breath and then shot out into space and headed for a bright object beyond a nearby moon. It stilled its wings and glided silently till it was drawn into the gently spinning lights of a massive corridor that hurtled the bird and its two tiny passengers to the far reaches of the universe and to the very edge of the Netherland itself. Here, they would find the basic laws of the universe changed.

WHERE IS THIS?

As it left the corridor, the bird expelled the air that it had stored in its lungs and started to breathe normally. This part of space was like no other they had ever encountered. It was no longer black, but full of white light. They could see planets and stars, but they themselves were lit up in the brightness. This overwhelming light was coming from somewhere in the far distance but it was not from a sun, as it was not giving any heat.

Lit up, right before Tommy and the goblin, spun a planet that was the jewel of the entire universe. It was the greatest achievement of a master creator and nothing could equal its beauty. It had oceans

of emerald green and turquoise blue and its lands were awash with vegetation that ran in huge swathes of different colours across its plains. Tommy particularly noticed that the lower slopes of its yellow- and scarlet-capped mountains were covered in the purple colour of kings.

As they finally landed, they felt fresh on their faces the tiny droplets of water that were rising high into the sky to form a circling mist that caused huge rainbows to arch across the sky. On the mountains many waterfalls came down, taking on the colours of the rocks through which they had trickled. Tommy took his shoes off and stood respectfully on the special ground. He knelt down and touched the cool water of a rippling stream and tasted its purity, then stood quietly to listen for the singing of the birds or the call of an animal from in the woods, but he heard nothing except the gentle whistle of the breeze and the babbling of the water in the stream.

'I have never heard such a silence,' he muttered.

'I know what you mean.' The goblin paused before he continued, 'Tommy, it is silent because there is no animal life here, not a fish in the sea nor a bird in the air – there is absolutely nothing at all.'

Tommy turned in disbelief. 'If there is no animal life, then what use is any of this beauty?'

The reply was whispered. 'They come here, The Mighty One and the Prince and a Spirit moves across the sky, and they remember.'

The goblin's gaze seemed to look far away.

'Remember what?' asked Tommy.

'That this was the alternative to creating life, to create no living thing at all, ever. Then there could never be any suffering or despair, never any pain or any death – a cruel word could never be spoken nor a true friend betrayed, never a wicked act or an evil deed. So, you can make your beautiful worlds and choose not to put a living thing in them, then sit and look at the work of your hands; but they will never talk to you and they will never know you have made them. You will stand among wonders and still be completely alone. Yes, this is the most beautiful planet in the universe, and it is also the loneliest!'

'But – he could make people who were good!'

'Oh,' replied the goblin, 'you mean he could programme them

like robots. I wonder what a conversation with a robot would be like.'

Tommy said, very quietly, 'I understand.'

As they climbed back on to the bird to leave the dreadfully lonely place, the goblin wondered why Tommy was being shown all these things. Why was it important for him to understand, and what place could he possibly have in the battle that was still to come?

THE LAND OF THE GIANTS

The bird rose high into white space and headed quickly out into the void. The two companions had much time to gather their thoughts and to admire the many different planets that passed as they travelled towards the reddish light of a distant sun.

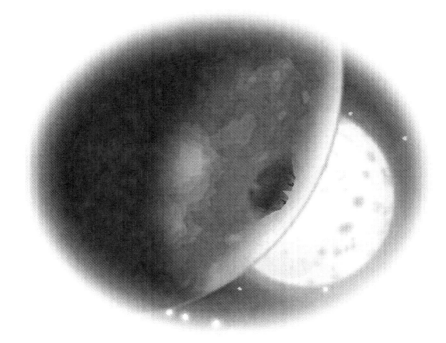

As they felt its ever-warmer rays, the bird banked steeply to the left and headed for a gigantic world that seemed very bright on one side. As it spun on its back, they saw the other side was in perpetual gloom. As they came closer, a giant mountain came into view on the edge of the dark side that, at its highest point, split into two frost-covered peaks that faced each other over a small divide. A great valley with sparse brown vegetation lay many miles below.

This was the legendary Land of the Giants on the Planet of Despair. The dark side was lit by three small moons but, as they came round, a fourth, huge moon came into view that lit up the mountain and gave the whole of the dark side an eerie and spectral light. As they landed on a plateau on the mountain's heights, the goblin explained the whole amazing fable to an excited Tommy.

'I have only heard of this in legend,' the goblin said. 'I did not know it was real, but it is all as I have been told. This whole world is a shrine; it is a monument to unrequited love.'

Tommy was puzzled. 'What is unrequited love?' he asked.

'It is a love that is unwanted and not returned. This whole place teaches you that love can blossom like a rose, or it can die in the place that it falls. Unrequited love can destroy not only your body;

it can also destroy your soul. This is not a place of fairy tales, but a place that shows you the truth. There is beauty and there is brutality here. Here love can stand you on the peaks of the highest mountain, or it can throw you in despair down to the deepest pit. This is the ice world of two lost souls.'

The goblin looked into Tommy's eyes. 'It is very hard to leave someone you love, Tommy,' he added.

As the goblin finished talking, the music from a gently played lament came floating around the side of the mountain.

'That will be the Keltians; they are the keepers of the shrine. They are calling us to go to them,' he said.

Deep frost crunched beneath their feet as they moved around the slope to a warm fire that never went out and towards two tall white-haired Keltians who were waiting to receive them. Tommy noticed that they were standing on the slopes of one of the two peaks at the very top of the mountain.

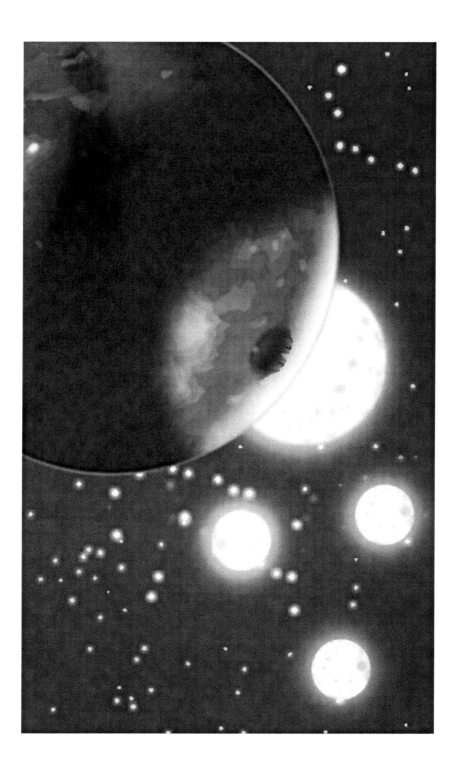

One Keltian talked to them, while the other began to play the same haunting lament they had heard before.

'We are the keepers of this ice world,' said the Keltian. 'We hold it in trust for the giants of Calis. Every year their young people come here to sing their songs of love. The females stand on the far slope, covered by the shadows, but the young men stand here in the full light of the giant moon. Great fires are lit to keep everyone warm, till all the songs have been sung. It is a celebration of love. It was always a perfect festival that ended with a huge feast given by the elders back in the home world of Calis, but one day it all started to go terribly wrong. As both choirs sang, one young Calistian called Cen continued to long for the young girl that he could only faintly see on the far slope.

'At the close of the songs, as everyone was gathered around the fires, he came and stood beside Sheban to tell her of his love. She reacted with scorn and disdain; her venomous hatred of him was there for all to see! Humiliated and in total despair, every eye now upon him, he travelled back through the corridor in disgrace. Unable to rest, he disappeared into the night, but was not missed till the next day. One girl, Esherra, had always cared deeply for Cen and this had turned into love. As he did not love her she had been unable to comfort him, but on hearing of his disappearance, she guessed at where he had gone. She raced to the corridor and back to the two peaks of the ice world, but was unable to find him for a long time. As she turned a corner by a huge rock, she saw him.

'He was kneeling on the ground, his head lifted up to the heavens and his body frozen in time. Mortified, and with hatred for Sheban burning through her body, Esherra knelt down before him till her body stiffened and her glazed eyes could no longer see. Her friends, desperately searching for her in her own world, finally realised what had happened and they too raced for the ice world.

'What they saw would live with them for ever. They left the tragic scene untouched and returned home in great sadness. It was the end of the age of innocence – their world was now tainted and unclean!'

At this, the Keltian put out her hand to point them in the direction of a far rock. 'Please approach, with respect and silence, the shrine of Esherra and Cen.'

Slowly the visitors walked up the slope and turned the far corner of the rock. There they stopped and stared in horrified silence at the sight that lay before them.

Two giant figures, their sparkling and frosted forms lit up by the moon and casting long shadows, were slouched, frozen, and face to face. His sightless eyes were looking up to the heavens and his love on the planet Calis, while Esherra's frozen stare was looking only at him – two heart-broken figures both looking to the one that they could not have.

After a long pause, and in great sadness, Tommy and the goblin walked back down to the Keltian. She again bowed to them. 'Your travelling-bird has flown,' she said. 'It couldn't stay long in the cold, but if you walk back to the plateau the light balls will take you to a side corridor and from there you may rejoin the main corridor back to Earth. May all your times be pleasing to you, Special One.'

Tommy thought for a moment that the keltian was talking to the goblin, but she was actually talking to him. They returned the shawls and walked tearfully away.

INTO THE FORBIDDEN WORLD

As they waited, two streaks of brilliant green light came racing across the sky and then hurtled down towards them. They slowed in only a second to the crawl that would allow their intended passengers to gather them up. Then Tommy and the goblin were away, up high through the stratosphere as the turbo-charged flyers zoomed back into white space.

As they approached a green corridor Tommy noticed a faraway corridor of brilliant white that ran straight and true towards the unknown source of light. Fascinated, he tried to move the green ball to go in that direction, but it resisted him and continually moved back towards the green corridor. It took a mighty effort and all his strength to hold his hand constantly in the direction of the white glowing corridor, but he imposed his will on the ball in his hand and was eventually moved towards it. As the two balls always travelled together, the goblin was forced to follow reluctantly.

As they arrived at the tunnel, they could see faint figures of people travelling inside being pulled silently by the power of an unseen hand, but there was no entrance and where it started or finished they could not see, so Tommy travelled along the outside towards the great light as the goblin marvelled and trembled at the little boy's bravery. The corridor eventually reached and went through a wall of blinding light, the people inside having reached their destination on the other side.

The goblin looked at the wall in awe. 'We have reached the very walls of Heaven. These people are being transported into paradise.' For a moment even Tommy felt overcome.

Tommy and the goblin could not follow, although they could make out the many people and the wonders that lay on the other side of the opaque wall. As they moved along the wall a golden hue seemed to stream through and the forms of many people could be dimly seen standing before a glowing building on whose front steps sat figures that were too bright to see.

'If only the wall was clear and we could see what we were looking at,' said Tommy. His frustration was boiling over and he had spoken loudly, which made the goblin very afraid and he started to move away. In front of the two figures, and lit up in the radiance, a dark figure was waving its arms about in a rage and seemed to be shouting abuse and making terrible threats to the two that sat on the thrones. It was during its furious insults that Tommy had spoken and the reaction of this sinister creature was instantaneous. It had immediately stopped and turned to look towards the wall. It then started to move ever closer and peered hard through the wall trying to see Tommy and the goblin who, by now, were finding this attention extremely unwelcome.

As the dark figure suddenly darted off in the direction of the corridor, Tommy and the goblin both panicked and held out their hands to get away before this monster could reach them.

The corridor became a blur to them as figures now going in the opposite direction zipped past, but one figure in the corridor was going in the same direction and he was nearly keeping up with them.

Distraught and frightened for their lives, they passed the corridor's entrance as souls from other worlds were being gently drawn into it. The souls, who were now on their final journey to the Netherland, could not even see the snarling figure that shot past them; but he was too late, for now back in normal space, he spotted the two figures disappearing into the main corridor and back towards the Earth. As the green light balls passed him on their way back, he fumed in anger. He would never be able to catch them now, as all light balls travelled faster than he could. He had tried to grab a light ball once, but he had quickly let go when it had burned his hand.

He suddenly remembered what Dego had said: the legion were camped at Mars, waiting for the Earth boy's return, so all was not lost. But how was he to treat this little being of flesh and blood? He didn't even know why the boy was important – and who or *what* was the goblin?

Taking the fearsome scowl off his face, he travelled on in the direction his retreating quarry had just taken.

WHAT A NICE MAN!

Tommy and the goblin screamed in terror and called for the agonisingly slow light balls to hurry up through the helix nebula and pick them up. They were alone and stranded in space at the mouth of the corridor, looking in horror at its entrance in expectation of a wild-eyed beast of fury rushing out.

As the first ball arrived, the goblin insisted Tommy took it, but the boy held back with his hand closed till they were both able to leave. For the first time, Tommy longed for the safety of home, and he held on grimly as he was hurtled back through the Kuiper belt, past the rings of Saturn and then more slowly through the asteroid belt, till both light balls came to a crunching halt in full view of Mars.

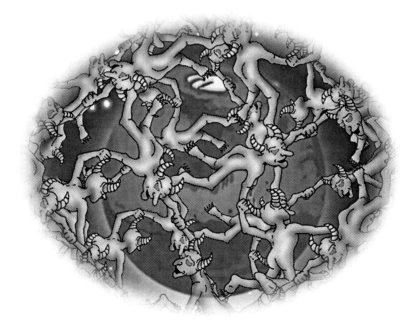

The sight that greeted him made him once again fear for his life. A huge army of spirits formed a barrier so high and so wide that it could not be passed. It was no longer possible to gain the speed that would take them clear of their enemies, who now roared and screamed with their hands raised high over their heads as they chanted unknown words.

As the army closed in, it suddenly went very quiet. Each spirit bowed and then knelt, with its hands held outward, as if in some form of worship.

'Oh no, oh my God, God help me!' screamed the goblin. Tommy turned round to see what had frightened him, but the creature that had come to stand behind them was not what Tommy expected. He was a tall, beautiful and angelic-looking being with an aura of white light all around him that gave the appearance of out-stretched wings. His skin shone so brightly that he lit up the space around him and his gentle smile and eyes of deep blue drew Tommy to approach him.

The angel was looking at him with great puzzlement. 'So, what have we got here? A troublesome little boy and a silly looking toy. Why would anyone want to bring you two out here? Unless the great prince wants you both to fight in his army…' The angel laughed. 'Do you want to fight in the great prince's army, Tommy?'

As Tommy did not understand what the angel had meant nor understood the question, he said nothing.

The glorious creature lowered itself to look into his eyes. 'Do you fear that mob over there?' It asked. 'They will not dare to harm you – no one will harm you while I stand by your side. Would you like to stand by my side and rule that army, Tommy?'

The thought of ruling an army of demons brought only a frown to the little boy's face – why would that appeal to him?

'Or perhaps,' the angel said quickly, 'you would rather rule a world? I can make you the ruler of an entire world, Tommy. I have the knowledge and the wisdom to teach you to lead many nations.'

'You shall lead them into great riches and freedom and herald the dawn of a new age. They shall no longer feel the need to bow down to a distant God and thank him for their hard-earned supper, or stand and sing songs in some meaningless ritual of worship. You will turn them into an independent people who can stand on their own feet and take by force what is rightfully theirs. You will oversee a golden age, where the spoil will go to the strong, and I shall be there, the power standing obediently by your right hand.'

And that was when the visions began! Tommy was now back home on the Earth, but the mirrors of the Parliament in which he stood showed him that he was now a young and charismatic man. He spoke, with great eloquence, to his nation's leaders who had become bemused by their many problems. His was a fresh and brilliant mind that could bring a nation together and gain the trust of its people as no one ever could before. Paraded by his peers on the world stage, he brought a new sense of one-world unity and brotherhood, making a clarion call to create a world fit for its future children and to eradicate the greed and corruption that had left the poor uncared for and unwanted! Every person who was presented to him, be they powerful and rich, or weak and poor, were afforded the same courtesy; it left them totally beguiled, putty in his hands. To lead them where they did not want to go he found easy and his praise was enough to take away the pain of the sacrifices he called on them to make. Soon the leaders of every nation had fallen under the spell of this man of vision, Tommy, who would save their world from the path of total destruction on which it had been set!

As the vision began to fade, he could see only happy and smiling faces waving flags of unity and listening intently to every word spoken on the screens that showed only his face.

As the visions ended, the angel spoke to him again. 'There are always some who will spoil the dream, so your power will be absolute and embrace your whole world.'

The words were spoken coldly and Tommy felt slightly alarmed as a cold shiver went down his spine. He barely had time to think before a new vision began.

Standing in the Temple of Dreams

Now he was standing in a great temple. It had huge columns of marble that rose hundreds of metres into the air, and the view down its steps showed people from every tribe on Earth walking along a tree-lined approach to lay tributes at its golden doors. This was the magnificent Temple of Dreams.

Those with great power and wealth were allowed to enter the heavily guarded doors and pay homage to its god who waited deep inside its holy place to receive their adoration. As Tommy stood in the deep recesses of the temple, the flickering flames of torches casting deep shadows all around, he looked up to a huge statue of the temple's god, which towered above him. Smiling kindly down on him from its lofty place was his own face – the face of Tommy Price! Now not only the great leader, he was also the god and object of worship, of every being on Earth. As he looked back in shock at the many faces before him, he saw that they were the faces of frightened and angry people who had been betrayed by this self-proclaiming deity – him!

Tommy saw only a blazing flash and felt the burning in his chest as he fell dazed to the floor, his lifeblood flowing out of him.

It was only the anger of the angel stood at his side and the voice of the goblin calling out to him that brought him out of his trance. The angel was enraged and shouted in fury, 'That is not the vision I meant for you! Somebody is interfering. I will resurrect you, you will live again. People will be astonished at you and will wonder at your supernatural powers. *That* is the truth, not this false vision of death! I will not take this interference, this is my space, I am God here!'

Above the ranting, Tommy could hear the goblin's desperate words, 'Tommy, he is not an angel, he is the Beast!'

The frightening figure of the Beast looked round, wild-eyed, for any sign of his interfering foe. Tommy backed away to stand by his friend as the beast ranted on, 'Lies, falsehoods! You will *never* die; you will conquer your world with the words that I will put in your mouth. Millions will listen to your every word and I shall teach you how to speak. Tell them what they want to hear and they'll believe every word you say, pretend you are honest and you'll get the power you want.'

Tommy was cringing. 'I cannot tell lies to gain power. Anyway, it might not work.'

The beast looked at him with disdain. 'Why not? It's always worked before. What are you – weak? Don't you *know* your own destiny?'

'I don't want my destiny to be with you!' shouted Tommy defiantly.

Now all pretence was gone as the creature screamed at him. 'You don't want your destiny to be with me? How dare you! Do you know who I am?'

The creature raised himself up to a towering height.

'I am Apollyon and Abaddon, the Dragon and the Serpent! I am Beelzebub, the Prince of the Power of the Air. I am the Goat of Mendez!'

As he spoke he became a goat with long horns, sitting upon a rock, his worshippers dancing round a fire in front of him. He stood up and approached Tommy, the light from the fire flickering in his eyes.

'I am the Bull of Bashan!' Suddenly, he became a powerful bull with fierce horns. It lowered its head and stamped its feet till the very heavens seemed to shake.

Then he returned to his first form and stood as a beautiful angel, who shone with more glory than the sun.

'I am Lucifer, fair as the morning. I am the Shining One, the bearer of light. I am the Prince of your world and ruler of all the Earth!'

But as he looked at a glaring Tommy, he realised the boy would never stand at his side. 'So, you are not my champion, you are his! So be it; I will find myself a champion, but I shall find him after you are dead. *My* living champion should beat *His* dead one, I think. So let that be your fate, little coward, to be *His* dead champion. What a waste! Destroy them, Dego!'

Any attack by the demons could frighten Tommy and the goblin to death but, seeing a new figure standing quietly behind the Beast, Dego stayed his hand.

'Master, it is the Great Prince,' Dego warned.

The Beast turned slowly to look with pure hatred into the face of his despised enemy. 'Just in time, Your Majesty. Your champion is about to die. You are good at that, are you not: suffering a weak and wishy-washy death instead of standing up to fight like a man? You just haven't got the bottle, have you?' he ranted.

The newcomer made no reply, but turned to Tommy and spoke to him in a calm and reassuring manner. The huge army that now prepared itself for attack seemed to hold little terror for him.

'Tommy, Shekencha, they cannot harm you. The only power they have is the power to deceive. What you see is what they have become. Trust me and face them without fear, I will tell you what to do.'

The goblin smiled, took Tommy's hand and they turned to face a horrific enemy, the sight of which should have struck them with terror. The newcomer had not impressed Tommy; he looked nothing like a great prince, but rather an ordinary and unremarkable man who had neither great stature nor a powerful presence.

The Beast beckoned his army to come and do its worst; the spirits coming in their thousands to stand across a small divide, cast insults and make gestures of death to their unprotected captives. Then, turning themselves into giant scorpions with stinging tails and razor-sharp claws, they raced, stingers raised, in full attack to frighten their enemy to death. They came from the direction of the sun, which lit them up and blinded Tommy and the goblin too much for them to look directly at the fearsome sight. Beside them, a huge black hole opened up in space that twisted and turned in a downward spiral into the depths of some unknown hell. Just as the scorpions were about to arrive, the two companions heard a voice of command.

Obediently, they opened out their hands to the sun; the light balls reflecting back the powerful rays to blind the incoming army, sending them hurtling into the abyss or blindly out into space.

The Beast himself moved away in dismay to gather up his scattered army. He would spend years finding and leading back those whom the black hole had flung to every corner of deep space.

Only Dego remained, looking back across the divide at the Great Prince with eyes very different to those of his scattered friends.

Tommy had been too confused to raise his hand at the word of command, but now saw the guardians appear who had done it for him. He was surrounded by many beautiful beings, who now held conference with the unremarkable man who seemed to lead them.

When the goblin went across and took the man's hand, tenderly talking to him, Tommy realised this really was the Great Prince. He had not recognised him because he was not shining as he had been when Tommy had seen him dimly through the barrier in the netherland.

The goblin was smiling, then started to bow and attempted to kneel, but the stranger only laughed and lifted him back up to talk to him as a friend.

Tommy looked back across the divide to where the demons had been, but now in the glare saw only one demon who, in lonely isolation, sadly turned and slipped quietly away. He felt relief and sadness at the man's final words, which were addressed to him: 'It is time for you to go home. My guardians will go with you and stay with you, but Shekencha must return to his own home. It is not yet time for us all to stand together, but we will, on the darkest and most glorious day in history. You shall see me looking for you, my friend, and I shall have need of you, so wait for me and be strong.'

Tommy could only look back in dismay as the man and his many guardians became smaller till they had disappeared from view and he was standing back in his own garden with the goblin beside him.

A corridor started to roar as it appeared and opened up only feet from the two of them and a guardian beckoned for the goblin to enter it.

The goblin turned sadly to look at Tommy, but then resolved to go home with a strong mind. He lifted his hand and waved goodbye.

'When will the Great Prince come?' Tommy called, but the slowly disappearing goblin did not know the answer.

'He will come in the sky, Tommy, so keep looking up to the sky,' the goblin replied.

'And the Beast – when will he come?'

He noticed the goblin's puzzled look and could only faintly hear his reply.

'The Beast… He is already here, Tommy, he is here!' And the goblin was gone.

All quiet now, and Tommy was totally alone! His front door creaked slowly open and he slipped inside the house into the gloom.

As he stood in the dark trying to gather his thoughts, he heard heavy breathing from just above him. A creature crouched, tongue hanging out, ready to pounce, launched itself from the stairs into the air and knocked him flat onto his back. Tail wagging furiously, it pinned him to the floor till he was quite unable to move.

'Oh, hello, Patch,' said Tommy cheerfully, 'and how are you?'

Printed in the United Kingdom
by Lightning Source UK Ltd.
123842UK00003B/130-240/A